19 × 10/07

This book belongs to ~~WITHDRAWN~~

_____

DISNEY'S TREASURE PLANET

A READ-ALOUD STORYBOOK

Adapted by Catherine Hapka
Illustrated by Judie Clarke, Adrienne Brown, Elena Naggi,
and the Disney Storybook Artists
Designed by Disney's Global Design Group
Cover painting by Dan Cooper

Random House 🏠 New York

For hundreds of years,
stories passed from spacer to
spacer of the notorious Captain
Nathaniel Flint and his band
of space pirates. The pirates had
looted merchant ships and kept their
vast treasure in a place so secret,
no one had been able to find it.
All that was known was that it lay
somewhere in the farthest reaches of
the galaxy . . . on a place called
Treasure Planet.

Fifteen-year-old Jim Hawkins lived on the rocky
planet of Montressor with his mother, Sarah. Life had
been difficult since Jim's father had left. His mother struggled
to provide for them by running a hotel and restaurant called the
Benbow Inn.

The only time Jim really felt free from all his worries was when
he was solar surfing. He loved performing board grabs, flips,
grinders, and other stunts.

"*Whoo-hoo!*" he shouted. Dipping and soaring through the air,
Jim had no idea that his entire life was about to change.

Crash! An alien ship fell to Montressor's surface. Jim raced over to see if he could help. But when he got there, he found a gravely injured alien pilot.

The alien's name was Billy Bones, and he had a warning for Jim.

"He's a-comin' . . . ," the turtle-like alien said with a hiss. "That fiendish cyborg and his band of cutthroats!"

Jim dragged the wounded alien through the door of the Benbow Inn. While Jim's mother and her friend Dr. Doppler watched, Billy Bones handed Jim a spherical object.

"He'll be comin' soon," Bones gasped. "I can't let him find this. . . ."

"*Who's* coming?" Jim asked.

"The cyborg! Beware the cyborg!" Billy Bones whispered with his last breath.

Just then, Jim looked out the window and saw a band of pirates charging toward the inn. Jim, Sarah, and Dr. Doppler barely escaped in Doppler's carriage as the pirates burned down the Benbow.

Later, safe inside Dr. Doppler's observatory, Jim began fiddling with the strange sphere. Suddenly the sphere opened and projected a large holographic map all around the room—a map to Treasure Planet!

Doppler and Jim set off to find the mysterious planet. The doctor hired a solar galleon and a crew of alien spacers. When he and Jim arrived at the spaceport, they stared in amazement.

"This is our ship!" Doppler said. "The RLS *Legacy*!"

On board, Jim and Doppler met Captain Amelia, a catlike alien, and Mr. Arrow, her sturdy first mate. The captain urged them not to show the map to anyone else on board.

"I don't much care for this crew you hired," she warned Dr. Doppler. "They are less than trustworthy."

Captain Amelia ordered Arrow to take Doppler and Jim down to the galley to meet the ship's cook, John Silver. Jim had been assigned to work as his cabin boy.

"Jimbo!" Silver said cheerfully, extending his mechanical hand. Jim gasped. He remembered Billy Bones's warning: *"Beware the cyborg!"*

"Now, don't be too put off by this hunk o' hardware," Silver said. "These gears have been tough gettin' used to, but they do come in mighty handy from time to time."

Jim also met Silver's pet, a protoplasmic shape-shifter named Morph.
"I rescued him on Proteus One," Silver said fondly, tickling Morph.
"We've been together ever since."

Doppler and Arrow went to prepare for the ship's launch. Jim was still thinking about Bones's warning.

"Just before I left Montressor," Jim said suspiciously, "I met this old guy who was, uh, kinda looking for a cyborg buddy of his. What was his name? Oh, yeah, Billy Bones."

Silver shrugged. "Musta been a different cyborg."

When Jim went upstairs to watch the launch, Silver said quietly to Morph, "We best be keepin' a sharp eye on this one, eh?"

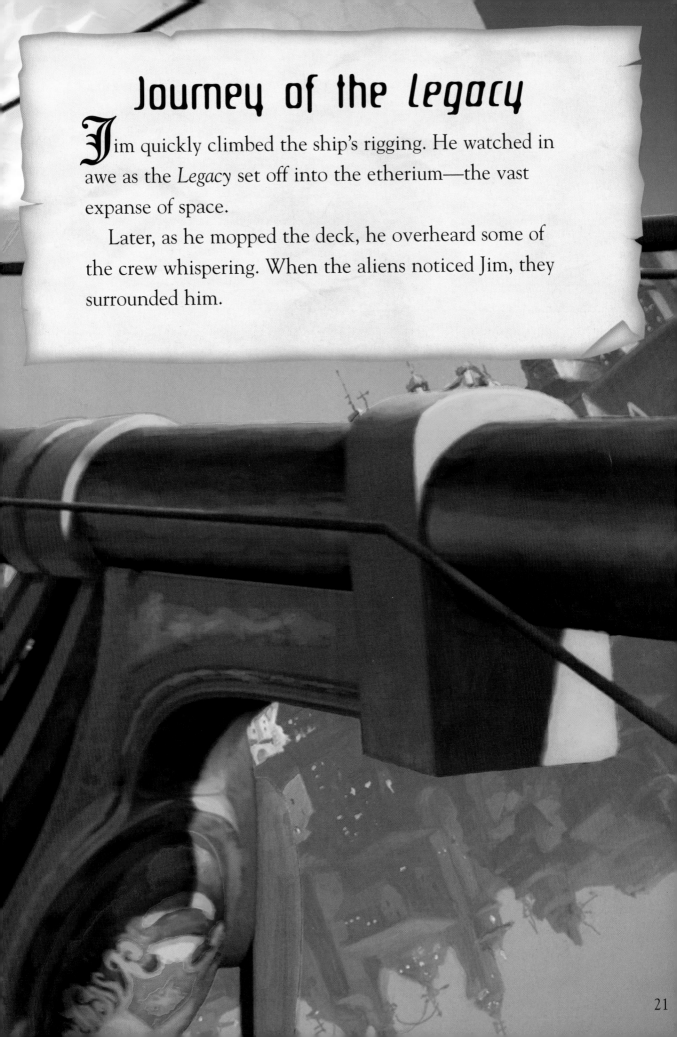

Journey of the Legacy

Jim quickly climbed the ship's rigging. He watched in awe as the *Legacy* set off into the etherium—the vast expanse of space.

Later, as he mopped the deck, he overheard some of the crew whispering. When the aliens noticed Jim, they surrounded him.

"Cabin boys should learn to mind their own business!" a spider-like alien named Scroop threatened, pushing Jim against the mast.

Luckily, Silver appeared just in time to save Jim.

Once Jim had left, Silver pulled the crew aside and quietly scolded them. "Ya want to blow the whole mutiny before it's time?" he said angrily. "Just stick to the plan. As for that boy, I'll run him so ragged he won't have time to think."

Over the next several weeks, Jim grew fond of the cyborg. Silver taught Jim everything he knew about ships—from cleaning barnacles off the hull to tying knots. Jim and Silver spent so much time together, they became almost like father and son.

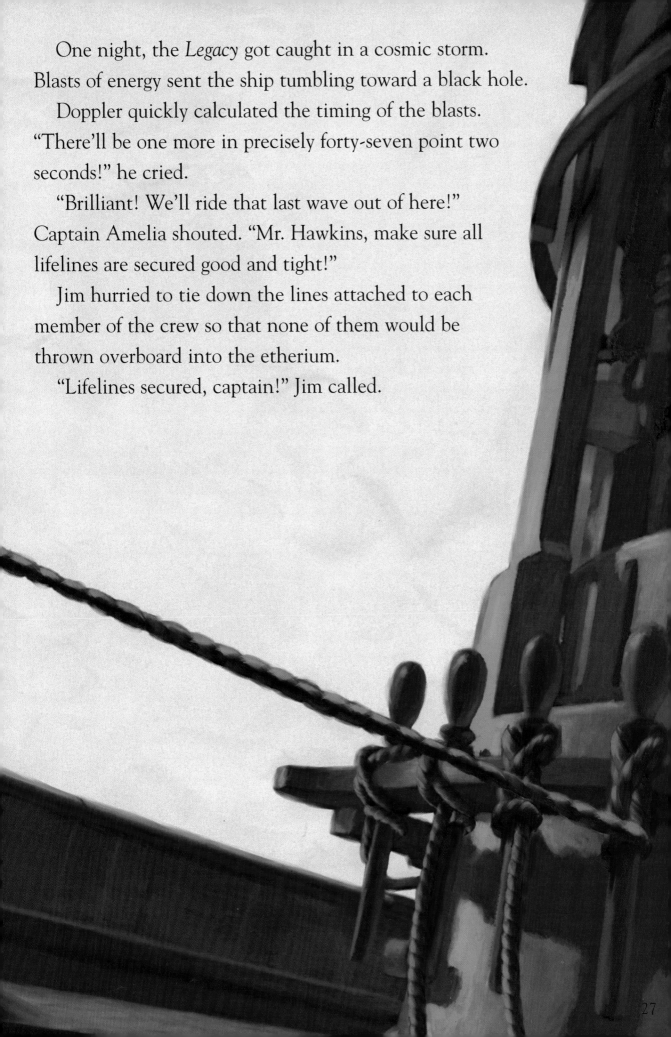

One night, the *Legacy* got caught in a cosmic storm. Blasts of energy sent the ship tumbling toward a black hole.

Doppler quickly calculated the timing of the blasts. "There'll be one more in precisely forty-seven point two seconds!" he cried.

"Brilliant! We'll ride that last wave out of here!" Captain Amelia shouted. "Mr. Hawkins, make sure all lifelines are secured good and tight!"

Jim hurried to tie down the lines attached to each member of the crew so that none of them would be thrown overboard into the etherium.

"Lifelines secured, captain!" Jim called.

With Doppler's help, Captain Amelia rode the next bumpy wave of energy out of the black hole. Soon the *Legacy* was safe.

"Well, I must congratulate you, Mr. Silver. It seems your cabin boy did a bang-up job with those lifelines," the captain said.

Silver patted Jim on the head. Jim was filled with pride, knowing that the captain and the cyborg were pleased with his work.

"All hands accounted for, Mr. Arrow?" the captain asked.

There was no answer. Arrow was gone!

Jim couldn't believe it. He *knew* Arrow's lifeline had been secured—he'd tied it himself! But no one believed him.

A little while later, Silver discovered that Scroop had cut Arrow's line! Silver felt terrible. But he couldn't tell Jim what had happened to Arrow without revealing his plan to mutiny. All he could do was try to convince Jim that he shouldn't blame himself.

"Ya got the makin's of greatness in ya!" Silver told Jim. "But ya gotta take the helm and chart yer own course."

The next morning, Morph playfully ran off with Jim's boot. Jim chased the little creature into a fruit barrel in the galley.

From inside the barrel, Jim overheard the crew having a secret meeting.

"We don't move till we got the treasure in hand," Silver said.

"I say we kill 'em all *now*!" Scroop argued. Then he accused Silver of having a soft spot for Jim.

"I care about one thing and one thing only—*Flint's trove*!" Silver answered angrily. "Ya think I'd risk it all for the sake of some nose-wipin' little whelp?"

Jim was crushed.

All of a sudden, a cry came from the deck. "Planet ho!"

The pirates ran upstairs to get their first glimpse of Treasure Planet. Jim scrambled out of the barrel.

But Silver spotted him. "Jimbo! Playin' games, are we?" he exclaimed grabbing Jim's arm.

Jim escaped from Silver's clutches and raced off to warn Captain Amelia and Dr. Doppler of the mutiny.

"Change in plan, lads! We move now!" Silver ordered his men when he reached the deck.

The pirates raised their flag and took over the ship.

In the captain's quarters, Amelia tossed the map to Jim. "Defend this with your life!" she ordered.

Jim, Doppler, and Amelia raced to the longboats to escape.

Morph thought it was all a game. He jumped out of Jim's pocket and took off—with the map!

Jim chased the little creature. Silver was right behind him. Spotting the sphere in a pile of coiled rope, Jim and Silver each tried to get to it first. Jim grabbed the map and dashed back to one of the longboats. He, Doppler, and Amelia took off.

The pirates fired a laser cannon at the escaping longboat.
"Hold your fire!" Silver shouted. "We'll lose the map!"
But it was too late! A laser blast ripped through the boat's mainsail. Captain Amelia managed to steer toward land. Moments later, the longboat crash-landed on Treasure Planet.

Captain Amelia was injured, but everyone was alive.

Jim was relieved to find that the map was still in his pocket. But suddenly he realized . . .

It was Morph! He'd turned himself into the map. That meant the *real* map was still back on the ship!

But the pirates were right behind them. They swooped down onto Treasure Planet in another longboat.

Captain Flint's Treasure

While Doppler stayed with Amelia, Jim and Morph looked for somewhere to hide.

Suddenly a strange figure leaped out of the bushes and hugged Jim. He introduced himself as B.E.N., Captain Flint's old navigational robot! Jim asked him about the treasure.

"I . . . I remember treasure . . . ," B.E.N. said, "buried in the centroid of the mechanism . . . DATA INACCESSIBLE! REBOOT!" The robot couldn't remember anything else because his primary memory chip had been removed.

B.E.N. couldn't help Jim and his friends find the treasure, but he *could* hide them from the pirates. He took them to his home.

It didn't take long for the pirates to find the friends' hiding place. Silver approached, waving a white flag of truce.

"Jimbo," Silver called, "I'd like a short word with ya."

"He's come to bargain for the map," Amelia guessed.

"That means he thinks we still have it!" Jim said. He agreed to meet with Silver.

"Whatever ya heard back there," Silver told Jim, "at least the part concerning you—I didn't mean a word of it. Listen, ya get me that map, and an even portion of the treasure is yours."

But Jim didn't trust Silver anymore. "I'm going to make sure you never see one drubloon of *my* treasure!" he told the pirate angrily.

"That treasure is owed me!" Silver cried furiously. He gave Jim until the next morning to hand over the map.

Jim knew he needed to go back to the *Legacy* and get the map. He, Morph, and B.E.N. stole one of the pirates' longboats and sneaked back to the ship.

Once on board, Jim and Morph raced to the coil of rope where Jim had last seen the sphere. It was still there! Jim grabbed the map and ran up the gangway to find B.E.N. All of a sudden, a sinister shadow appeared at the top of the stairs. It was Scroop!

While Jim struggled with Scroop, Morph got scared and ran away. On another part of the ship, B.E.N. accidentally deactivated the gravity field. Jim and Scroop floated up the ship's rigging, scrambling to find something to hold on to. Jim reached the rope and then grabbed hold of the ship's sturdy mast, but Scroop wasn't so lucky. He went spinning out into space, never to be seen again!

Jim, Morph, and B.E.N. returned to Treasure Planet—and found the pirates waiting for them! The pirates had already captured Doppler and Amelia. Silver grabbed the sphere, but he couldn't figure out how to open it.

"You want the map, you're taking me, too," Jim told him.

"We'll take 'em all," Silver said to the pirates.

A little while later, the longboat landed on a winding jungle path. A pirate stayed on board to guard Doppler and Amelia as Jim used the map to lead the rest of the group closer to the treasure. At last they reached the edge of a cliff.

"What's goin' on, Jimbo?" Silver asked as the map suddenly closed, returning to its sphere shape.

Thinking Jim had misled them, one of the pirates pushed him to the ground. There Jim came face to face with a circular pattern on the edge of the cliff. He put the sphere in the middle of it.

With a flash of light, a holographic image and a huge triangular portal appeared. The image was a controller that allowed spacers to travel instantly between planets.

"So that's how Flint did it!" Jim said. "He used this portal to roam the universe stealing treasure."

"Treasure . . . treasure . . . ," B.E.N. started to say, clutching his head. "It's buried in the . . ."

". . . centroid of the mechanism!" Jim finished, remembering what B.E.N. had babbled earlier. The treasure must be in the center of the planet! He placed his finger in the middle of the controller, and with a brilliant flash, the portal opened to reveal a huge chamber.

Jim and the pirates stepped through the portal. There were mountains of glittering treasure everywhere—and Flint's ship was perched atop the highest heap!

"The loot of a thousand worlds," Silver whispered. "At last . . ."

Jim hurried to Flint's ship. If he could only start the engines, they could escape! On the ship, he found Flint's skeleton holding something in its bony fist. Jim looked more closely. It was B.E.N.'s missing memory chip!

"It's all flooding back!" B.E.N. exclaimed when Jim inserted the chip. "All my memories! Right up until Flint pulled my memory circuit so I could never tell anybody about his . . . booby trap!"

Then there was a huge rumble. The chamber began to shake. All the pirates rushed to the portal to try to escape—except for Silver.

"Run, Jimmy!" B.E.N. shouted.

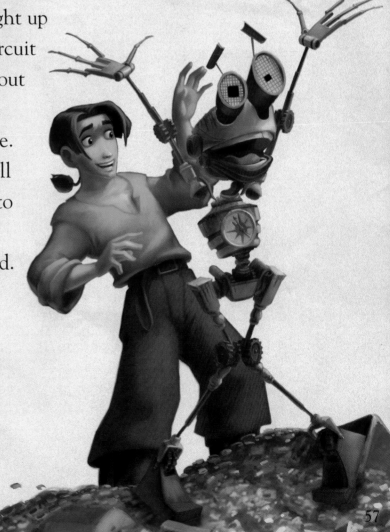

But Jim was determined to start Flint's ship. Just as the engines roared to life, Silver jumped onto the ship, too. Jim tried to force him off with one of Flint's swords. Suddenly, the ship lurched forward, throwing Jim and Silver overboard! Silver grabbed the rail, but Jim lost his footing and fell down a steep slope.

Silver was holding the ship so it wouldn't drift into one of the

energy beams that were ripping the planet apart. But when he saw
Jim about to fall into a deep hole, he shouted, "Jimbo! Reach for me
now! *Reach!*"

But it was no use. Silver could not reach Jim—even with his
mechanical arm fully extended! He would have to let go of the
ship—and his dreams of treasure—to save Jim.

"Oh, blast me for a fool," Silver said, letting go of the ship to grab Jim's arm and pull him to safety.

Together they watched the treasure-filled ship disappear forever as it was sucked into a destructive energy beam. Then Jim and Silver jumped through the portal and joined the others, who had already made it back to the *Legacy*.

But it wasn't safe there, either. Treasure Planet was exploding, and the *Legacy* did not have the power to escape in time!

"We gotta turn around!" Jim shouted. "There's a portal back there that can get us outta here!" With Silver's help, he put together a makeshift solar surfer and took off. At the last second he reached the triangular portal. With one touch of the controller, Jim helped the *Legacy* hurtle through the portal to safety.

"Ya done it, Jim!" Silver exclaimed. "Didn't I say the lad had greatness in him?"

A little while later, Jim found Silver in the ship's longboat bay. The cyborg was trying to escape before Amelia could send him to prison. "What say ya ship out with us, lad?" Silver asked Jim.

Jim let his friend go free but decided not to join him. "I met this old cyborg who taught me that I could chart my *own* course," Jim said. For the first time in his life, Jim saw a future in front of him . . . a bright future.

The etherium remains a place filled with hidden treasures, but for one young lad, it became a place of great discovery, too. For it was there that he found a place called Treasure Planet, and it was there that he met a bold space pirate who taught him that the greatest treasure of all was buried where he least expected it—inside himself.